To Anna, Franklin, and Olivia

With special thanks to my editor, Mary Kate Castellani,
and to the KTM group. Your wisdom and support
always soothe my tummy.

First published in the United States of America in July 2015 by Bloomsbury Children's Books
www.bloomsbury.com

Bloomsbury is a registered trademark of Bloomsbury Publishing Plc

For information about permission to reproduce selections from this book, write to
Permissions, Bloomsbury Children's Books, 1385 Broadway, New York, New York 10018
Bloomsbury books may be purchased for business or promotional use. For information on bulk purchases
please contact Macmillan Corporate and Premium Sales Department at specialmarkets@macmillan.com

Library of Congress Cataloging-in-Publication Data
Wohnoutka, Mike, author, illustrator.
Dad's first day / by Mike Wohnoutka.
pages   cm
Summary: Oliver and Dad have spent a fun summer together, but when it comes time for the first day of school,
Dad discovers that he is not ready and does everything he can to postpone the big day.
ISBN 978-1-61963-473-2 (hardcover)
ISBN 978-1-61963-745-0 (e-book) · ISBN 978-1-61963-746-7 (e-PDF)
[1. Fathers and sons—Fiction. 2. First day of school—Fiction. 3. Humorous stories.] I. Title.
PZ7.W81813Dad 2015   [E]—dc23   2014022105

Art created with Holbein Acryla gouache paint
Typeset in Sassoon Sans Std and Draftsman Casual
Book design by Amanda Bartlett

Printed in China by Leo Paper Products, Heshan, Guangdong
2 4 6 8 10 9 7 5 3 1

Dad's First Day

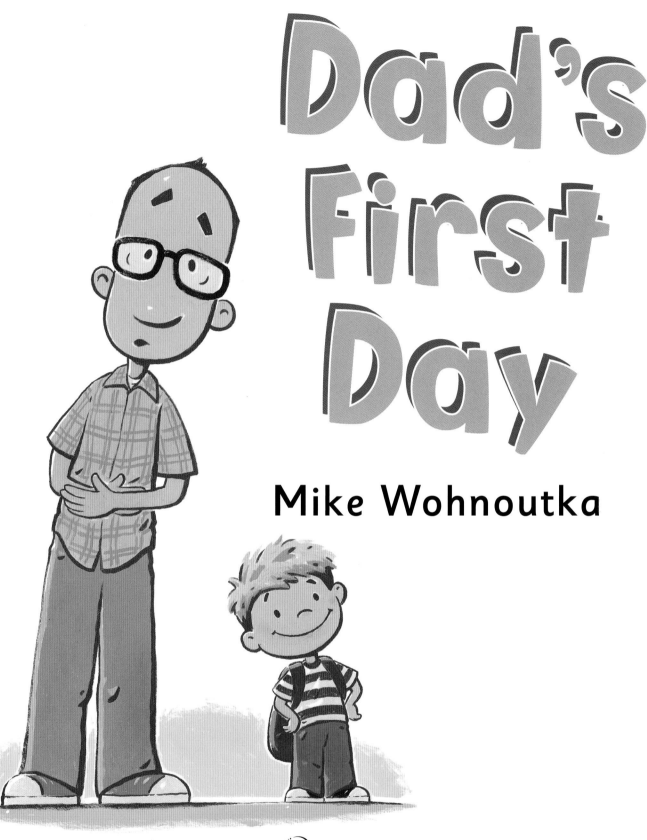

Mike Wohnoutka

BLOOMSBURY

NEW YORK   LONDON   NEW DELHI   SYDNEY

This is Oliver.
And this is Oliver's dad.

All summer they
played together,

laughed together,

sang together,

and read
together.

When summer was over, it was time for Oliver to start school.

Are you ready for school?

Yes!

The night before school started, Oliver and his dad got ready.

On the first day of school,
Oliver's dad didn't feel good.

My tummy hurts.

It's okay, Daddy, you're just a little nervous.

Come on, let's go— we don't want to be late for the first day of school!

But Oliver's dad had a few things he needed to do before they left.

Daddy! What are you doing?
We need to go now!

So Oliver's dad . . .

. . . hid behind the couch.

Oliver found him.

He hid inside the closet.

Oliver found him.

He hid outside.

Daddy!

Oliver found him and
dragged him to the car.

Oliver's dad drove very slowly.

You're probably going to really miss me when you're at school, Oliver.

Sure, Daddy.

When they got to school, Oliver ran to his classroom and met his teacher.

So nice to meet you, Oliver!

My tummy really hurts.

Then it was time to say good-bye.

Bye, Daddy.

Daddy?

Daddy.

Daddy!

Bye, Daddy!

The teacher walked Oliver's dad outside.

Oliver's dad drove home.

He couldn't stop thinking about Oliver.

He worried about Oliver. He missed Oliver.
And his tummy *really*, *really* hurt.

Then he
realized . . .

I'm not ready for school!

Oliver's dad drove back to the school.

He ran to the classroom.

And just before he opened the door, he stopped.

He couldn't believe what he saw.

Oliver was playing.

He was laughing.

Then he was singing and reading.

Oliver's dad . . .

. . . smiled.

Oliver *and* his dad were ready for school.

Good job,
Daddy!

After the first day of school,
they celebrated . . .
until their tummies hurt.